fairytale Collection

Published in the United States by Random House Children's Books, a division of Random House, Inc., 1745 Broadway, New York, NY 10019, and in Canada by Random House of Canada Limited, Toronto.

The works in this collection were originally published separately in the United States by Random House Children's Books as *Barbie: Fashion Fairytale*, copyright © 2010 Mattel, Inc.; *Barbie in a Mermaid Tale*, copyright © 2010 Mattel, Inc.; *Barbie and the Three Musketeers*, copyright © 2009 Mattel, Inc.; *Barbie: Thumbelina*, copyright © 2009 Mattel, Inc.; and *Barbie and the Diamond Castle*, copyright © 2008 Mattel, Inc.

Step into Reading, Random House, and the Random House colophon are registered trademarks of Random House, Inc.

Visit us on the Web!
StepIntoReading.com
www.randomhouse.com/kids
www.barbie.com

Educators and librarians, for a variety of teaching tools, visit us at
www.randomhouse.com/teachers

ISBN: 978-0-375-87255-6

MANUFACTURED IN CHINA
10 9 8 7 6 5 4

Dear Parent:

Congratulations! Your child is taking the first steps on an exciting journey. The destination? Independent reading!

STEP INTO READING® will help your child get there. The program offers five steps to reading success. Each step includes fun stories and colorful art. There are also Step into Reading Sticker Books, Step into Reading Math Readers, Step into Reading Phonics Readers, Step into Reading Write-In Readers, and Step into Reading Phonics Boxed Sets—a complete literacy program with something to interest every child.

Learning to Read, Step by Step!

Ready to Read   Preschool–Kindergarten
• big type and easy words • rhyme and rhythm • picture clues
For children who know the alphabet and are eager to begin reading.

Reading with Help   Preschool–Grade 1
• basic vocabulary • short sentences • simple stories
For children who recognize familiar words and sound out new words with help.

Reading on Your Own   Grades 1–3
• engaging characters • easy-to-follow plots • popular topics
For children who are ready to read on their own.

Reading Paragraphs   Grades 2–3
• challenging vocabulary • short paragraphs • exciting stories
For newly independent readers who read simple sentences with confidence.

Ready for Chapters   Grades 2–4
• chapters • longer paragraphs • full-color art
For children who want to take the plunge into chapter books but still like colorful pictures.

STEP INTO READING® is designed to give every child a successful reading experience. The grade levels are only guides. Children can progress through the steps at their own speed, developing confidence in their reading, no matter what their grade.

Remember, a lifetime love of reading starts with a single step!

STEP INTO READING®

STEP 2

Barbie™
fairytale Collection

Barbie in A Mermaid Tale

Barbie A Fashion Fairytale

Barbie and The Three Musketeers

Barbie The Diamond Castle

Barbie Thumbelina

Step 2 Books

A Collection of Five Early Readers

Random House 🏠 New York

Contents

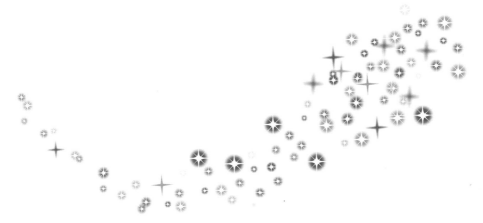

Barbie™
A Fashion Fairytale

Adapted by Mary Man-Kong

Based on the original screenplay by Elise Allen

Illustrated by Dynamo Limited

Random House 🏠 New York

Barbie is
on a plane.
She is going to Paris.
Her pet poodle
is going,
too.
They will help
Barbie's Aunt Millicent.

Millicent is happy
to see Barbie.
But Millicent is sad,
too.
Her fashion house
is closing forever.

Jacqueline is
a mean dressmaker.
She stole Millicent's
fashion ideas.

Alice is
Millicent's helper.
She makes pretty
dresses.
She does not want
Millicent's store
to close.

Barbie and Alice
find a secret wardrobe.

Glimmer, Shimmer,
and Shyne come out.
They are the Flairies!
Their magic makes
Alice's dress sparkle.

Alice and Barbie
love it!

A lady buys
the sparkling dress.
Barbie has an idea.

They will have
a fashion show.
They will
save Millicent's!

Alice and Barbie
work hard.
They make
lovely dresses.

The Flairies make the dresses extra pretty!

Jacqueline wants
the Flairies
to make <u>her</u> dresses
sparkle.

She and her helper kidnap the Flairies!

But the Flairies do not
like Jacqueline's dresses.
The magic will not last.

Jacqueline plans her own
fashion show anyway.

Barbie and Alice are done!

Millicent loves
their dresses.

The Flairies are trapped.
They light up
Jacqueline's store.

The pets save them!

Glimmer, Shimmer,
and Shyne are free!

Jacqueline starts
her fashion show.
But the magic
stops working.

Her fashions turn
into trash!
The show
is a flop.

Millicent starts
her fashion show.
Many people come.

Barbie peeks
at the crowd.
Alice knows Barbie
will be a great model.

Barbie walks
down the runway.
The Flairies make
Barbie's dress
glimmer, shimmer,
and shine.

Millicent's fashion show
is a hit!

Barbie and her friends
thank the Flairies.
Together,
they saved Millicent's
fashion house!

Barbie in A Mermaid Tale

Adapted by Christy Webster
Based on the original screenplay by Elise Allen
Illustrated by Ulkutay Design Group
and Pat Pakula

Random House 🏠 New York

Merliah loves to surf.
She is the best surfer
in Malibu.

Merliah's hair turns
pink!
She dives
underwater.
She can breathe!

Merliah meets Zuma.

Zuma is a dolphin.

Zuma talks!

Zuma tells Merliah
about her past.
Merliah is half
mermaid!

Merliah's mother was
a mermaid named
Calissa.

Merliah's mother
gave her a necklace.

Merliah does not
believe Zuma.
She smashes
the necklace.

Mermaid magic
comes out.
It shows them
Merliah's mother.
She is in trouble.

"Please help her,"
Zuma says.

Merliah agrees.

They swim deep
into the ocean.

Merliah and Zuma
go to Oceana.
It is a pretty city
underwater.

Calissa is the true
queen of Oceana.
But Merliah's evil
aunt Eris is now queen.
She keeps Calissa
in prison.

Two mermaids
give Merliah
a fake tail.

They will help Merliah.

So will Snouts.

He is a baby sea lion.

Merliah goes
to the Destinies.
They tell fortunes.

They tell her
to do three tasks.
Then she can beat Eris.

Merliah climbs high.
She does
the first task.

She finds
the magic comb!

Now Merliah must
find a dreamfish.
Zuma knows where to go.

Eris's manta sharks
chase them.
They must escape!

Merliah surfs
a huge current.
She meets
a dreamfish!

The dreamfish
loves Merliah's surfing.
He will help her.

Merliah has
one more task.
She needs Eris's
necklace.

Merliah has a plan.

She grabs the necklace!

Eris is angry.

Eris traps Merliah
in a whirlpool.

Merliah accepts that
she is a mermaid.
She gets a real
mermaid tail!

Merliah escapes!
Eris is trapped
in the whirlpool
instead.
Oceana is saved!

Calissa is free!
Merliah finally
meets her mother.
Calissa gives Merliah
a new magic necklace.
Merliah has a home
in both worlds!

STEP INTO READING®

STEP 2

Barbie™ and The Three Musketeers

Adapted by Mary Man-Kong

Based on the original screenplay by Amy Wolfram

Illustrated by Ulkutay Design Group and Allan Choi

Random House 🏠 New York

Corinne loves to fence.
She wants to be
a Musketeer.
She wants to protect
the royal family.

Corinne goes to Paris.
She learns that she
cannot be a Musketeer.

A dog chases
Corinne's kitten.
Corinne runs after them.
They splash past Viveca.

Corinne bumps
into Aramina.

Renée falls

into the water.

Corinne finds her kitten
near the castle.

Corinne meets the girls
she splashed, bumped,
and knocked over!

They forgive her.

Corinne gets a job
at the castle.

She is a maid.

She meets Prince Louis.

He is going to be king.

Philippe is Louis's cousin.

Philippe is angry.

He wants to be king.

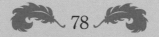

Prince Louis is
in danger.

Crash!

The roof caves in!

Corinne smashes rocks.

Viveca cracks bricks.

Aramina kicks stones.
Renée breaks blocks.
Everyone is saved!

The girls want
to protect the prince.

They want to be
Musketeers!
They use a secret room
to practice.

Prince Louis takes
his hot-air balloon
for a ride.
But someone cut the rope!
Corinne saves Louis.

Corinne and the prince float over Paris. They have fun together.

Philippe plans
to attack Louis.

The girls have a plan, too.
They will protect the
prince.

The girls go to
the royal ball.

Their gowns sparkle.
Their crowns shine.

Corinne dances
with the prince.

Philippe is going
to attack the prince!

The girls are ready!

Corinne uses her sword.

Viveca uses her ribbons.

Aramina uses her fans.

Renée uses her bow.

They stop the attack!

Corinne stops Philippe
with her sword.
The prince is safe!

Louis makes all
the girls royal
Musketeers.

All for one
and one for all!

STEP INTO READING®

STEP 2

Barbie™ Thumbelina

Adapted by Diane Wright Landolf

Based on the original screenplay by Elise Allen

Illustrated by Ulkutay Design Group and Allan Choi

Random House 🏠 New York

Thumbelina is tiny.
She made wings.
Her best friends,
Chrysella and Janessa,
watch her fly!

They are Twillerbees.
They all live
in a big field.

The three friends
try out their wings.
Then they hear a rumble.

It is humans!
Humans are coming
with their big trucks.

In one truck
rides a spoiled girl
named Makena.
"I want those flowers,"
she tells her parents.

As the friends watch,
a bulldozer comes close.
They need to hide!

When they come out,
they are in
a huge bedroom.
It is Makena's room.

Makena says her parents
will dig up the field
to build a factory.

Thumbelina is angry.

Chrysella and Janessa
fly back to the field
to warn the others.

Thumbelina stays.

She wants to try to stop

Makena's parents.

At the field,
Twillerbees work hard.
They use their magic
to make vines grow
all over the trucks!

The field is safe
for one more day.

Thumbelina asks Makena
to help save the field.
Makena agrees.

She asks her parents
not to build the factory.
They love Makena,
but they are busy.
They do not listen to her.

Thumbelina finds
an old drawing.
It shows Makena's family.

Later, Makena gives
Thumbelina a makeover.
Now they are
best friends.

Thumbelina makes
a garden for her friend.

It is just like the one
in the drawing.
Makena loves it.

Then Makena's
friend Violet comes over.
Thumbelina thinks
Makena just wants
to show her off.

Her feelings are hurt.

She flies home.

Makena bikes
to Twillerbee Field.

She says Thumbelina
is her only true friend.
She wants to help
save the field.
Thumbelina has a plan.

At Makena's house,
the Twillerbees make
the garden even better.

Makena leads her parents
to the garden.
She tells them
about the Twillerbees.
This time, they listen.

The family rushes
to the field.
Makena stands
in front of the trucks!

The work stops.

The field is safe.

The new friends enjoy
the field together.
It is a perfect day
for a picnic!

Barbie & The Diamond Castle

Adapted by Kristen L. Depken

Based on the original screenplay
by Cliff Ruby & Elana Lesser

Illustrations by
Ulkutay Design Group & Allan Choi

Random House 🏠 New York

Alexa and Liana
are best friends.
They love to sing.
One day,
they find magic stones.
They make necklaces.
They promise to be
best friends always.

Later that day,
Liana and Alexa meet
a poor old woman.

The girls give her
their lunch.
The woman gives them
an old mirror.

At home,

the girls sing.

A third voice joins in.

It is coming

from the mirror!

A girl named Melody

is trapped inside.

Melody tells the story
of the Diamond Castle.
Three muses lived there.
But evil Lydia wanted
to be the only muse.

The two good muses
hid the Diamond Castle.
They gave Melody the key.
Then Lydia turned
the good muses to stone.

Now Lydia wants the key
to the Diamond Castle.
Lydia's dragon, Slyder,
must find Melody.

Slyder flies
to the girls' cottage.
They hide in the cellar.
Slyder is right upstairs!
The girls all escape.

Melody still has the key.
She can save the muses.
Alexa and Liana
set out for the castle
with the mirror.

On the way,
they find two puppies.
They name them
Lily and Sparkles.

Soon the girls

meet twin brothers.

Their names are
Jeremy and Ian.
They want to help
Liana and Alexa.

Lydia and Slyder look
for Alexa and Liana.
Slyder chases them!

The twins rescue
the girls just in time!

Alexa and Liana
rest at a manor.
They find food to eat
and they try on gowns.

But the girls argue.

Alexa wants to stay.

Liana thinks

they should keep going.

Lydia lures both girls
to her cavern.
She puts Alexa
under a spell.

Alexa is
going to fall!
Liana and Lily
save her.
The girls are
friends again.

Now Lydia has
the mirror.
Melody is still inside!
Lydia creates
a whirlpool.

She uses a spell
to make the girls
walk into it.
But they trick her!

Alexa grabs
Lydia's magic flute.
Liana saves the mirror
from Lydia.

Alexa and Liana sing.
Then the Diamond
Castle appears!
Singing was the key!

Melody appears, too.
She is free
from the mirror!
The Diamond Castle
sparkles with magic.

Lydia and Slyder

turn to stone.

The good muses are free.

Liana and Alexa become
Princesses of Music.
Their gowns sparkle.
Liana, Alexa,
and Melody are
best friends always.